FEARLESS
FISH

GOOF-OFF
GOOSE

HEALTHY
HIPPO

IMITATING
IGUANA

JEALOUS
JACKAL

POSITIVE
PIG

QUESTIONING
QUAIL

RESPONSIBLE
RABBIT

SMARTY
STORK

TEMPER TANTRUM
TURTLE

HERE THEY ARE

SWEET PICKLES ®

All twenty-six of them
in stories with giggles
and tickles and awful pickles

YAKETY
YAK

ZANY
ZEBRA

Hefter   6/23/80

Very Worried Walrus

DATE DUE

NOV. 8	1980	NOV 7	1980	JUL	5 2001
NOV. 1 3 1980	AUG. 9	1984		
NOV. 22 1980	SEP. 1 5 1984		
DEC. 22 1980	NOV. 2 9 1984		
JAN. 2 4 1981	SEP. 7	1985	
FEB. 1 4 1981	APR. 5	1986	
MAR. 1 4 1981	MAY 5	1986	
APR. 1 4	NOV. 1	1986	
OCT. 2 8 1981	SEP. 1 0 1987		
DEC. 1 9 1981	JUN. 2 2 1990		
JAN. 3 1983	NOV. 2 8 1992		
	JAN 0 6 2000		

THIS

SWEET PICKLES ®

BOOK BELONGS TO

In the world of *Sweet Pickles*, each animal gets into a pickle because of an all too human personality trait.

This book is about Worried Walrus who worries a lot—especially about riding a bicycle.

Other Books in the Sweet Pickles Series

ME TOO IGUANA
STORK SPILLS THE BEANS
ZEBRA ZIPS BY
GOOSE GOOFS OFF
FIXED BY CAMEL

Library of Congress Cataloging in Publication Data

Hefter, Richard.
    Very worried walrus.

    (Sweet Pickles series)
    SUMMARY: Walrus would like to ride a bicycle but
worries about all that could happen if he fell.
    [1. Walruses–Fiction] I. Title. II. Series.
PZ7.H3587Ve3   [E]   76-43092
ISBN 0-03-018091-0

Printed in the United States of America

Weekly Reader Books' Edition

Weekly Reader Books presents

VERY WORRIED WALRUS

Written and Illustrated
by Richard Hefter
Edited by Ruth Lerner Perle

Holt, Rinehart and Winston · New York

"I'd really like to ride this bike," said Walrus. "But I'm afraid I'll fall off."

"No, you won't," said Pig. "Don't worry."

"There's a lot to worry about," sighed Walrus. "If I fall off, I'll get hurt. Then I'll have to go to the doctor. And I'll need medicine or bandages...or...stitches! Ohhh!"

"That's silly," laughed Pig. "Bicycle riding is fun and there is no reason to worry."

"That's all right for you to say," gulped Walrus. "You're not about to get up on this bicycle.

"There's so much to worry about when you're up on a bicycle. An awful lot can go wrong. You have to steer and pedal and balance. You have to look out in front of you and on both sides and make sure no one is behind you...and not go too fast...and use your brakes."

"And you can still crash and bump and fall and slip and slide and get hurt!"

"And if I get hurt, they'll have to take me to the hospital in an ambulance."

"I can see it now...there's a traffic jam on Main Street. The ambulance gets stuck. The driver radios the police to send a helicopter to get me out."

"When the helicopter arrives, there's no place to land, so the pilot lowers a rope.

"Then the ambulance driver ties my stretcher to the rope and the helicopter goes up."

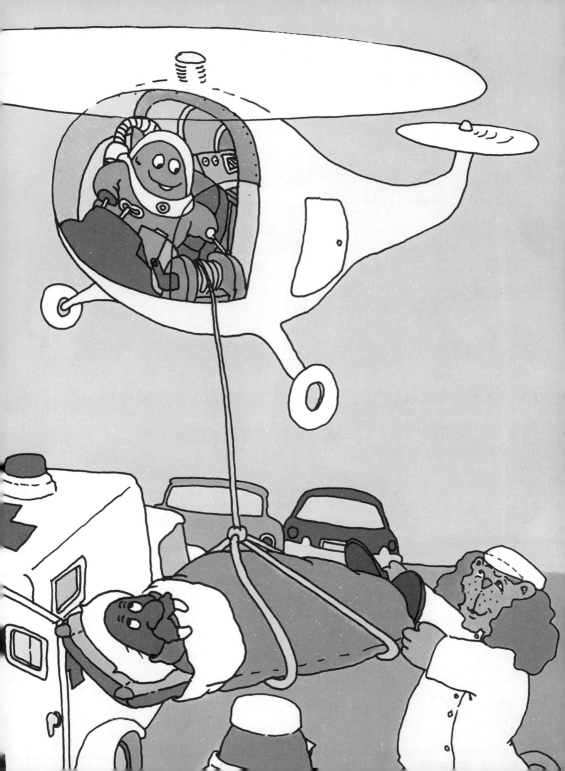

"Up and up and up, over the rooftops and out towards the river. There I am, hanging on the end of a rope attached to a helicopter flying over the water."

"And the rope snaps."

"Down I go. Down, down, down, splash! I'm in the river and it's cold.

"I swim and swim."

"Finally a tugboat passes by and it picks me up."

"But the tugboat is going in the wrong direction and by the
time I get off, I am miles away from home."

"And the last train has left. And the buses aren't running."

"So I start walking. And it's cold. And it's getting dark. And my sweater is dripping and my shoes are going splish, splosh, splish. Then it starts to rain, and I'm so tired, and it's really dark now, and I'm hungry, and there is nothing around. No houses, no people, nothing, and…."

"Hey, hey, hey, Walrus!" called Pig. "Stop worrying so much. It's a beautiful day. The sun is shining. The flowers are blooming. Think of the fun you'll have riding the bicycle!"

Walrus looked at Pig, then he looked at the bicycle. "Well, maybe," he said. "Maybe it will be all right. Maybe it will be. I guess I'll try."

Walrus got on the bicycle. He balanced. He pedalled. He looked ahead. He looked to the side.

"Whee!" he shouted. "This *is* fun."

He went faster.
He looked behind him.
He ran into a tree.

CRASH!

Walrus lay on the ground. He thought about the ambulance and the helicopter and the tugboat.

"Hey, Walrus!" called Pig. "You okay?"

Walrus stood up and brushed himself off. He looked down at his feet. He felt himself all over. Then he looked at Pig, and smiled.

"Don't worry," he said. "I'm fine!"

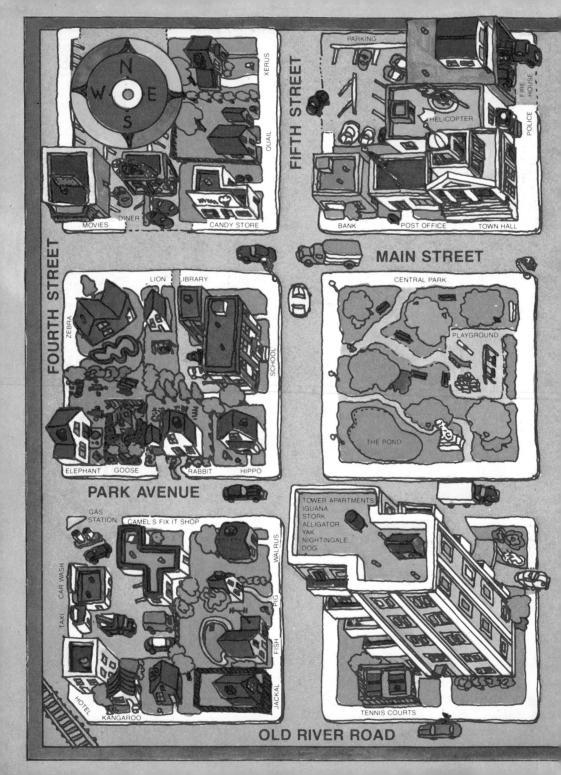